And if you look very closely
You may see a little house,
Too tiny for a hedgehog,
Too teeny for a mouse!

Here live The Tickle Misses!
Fairies hard at work and play,
Making dreams come true for you,
Adding sparkle to your day.

Here is Jessie to say hello,
Tickle Miss Scatterbrain!
But even though things may go wrong
She'll try and try again.

Sometimes when no-one's watching
She'll whizz around the dusky sky,
Sprinkling you with fairy dust,
And getting it in her eye!

Poppy is the Tickle Miss who
Loves beautiful, girly things:
Ribbons and lace and handbags and shoes,
Necklaces, bracelets and rings!

Jessie tells Poppy of the party plan.
Poppy is very excited!
She has beautiful blooms for decoration.
Jessie is delighted!

They sit in the sun, worn out by fun,
The sky above is so blue.
'What will you wear?' 'Flowers in your hair?'
There are so many things to do!

Jess says goodbye, it's time to go.
Invites are blown out of her hand!
Oh no, what a mess! Oh poor old Jess!
Confetti scattered all over the land!

Here comes Poppy to help poor Jess,
They flutter and whizz around,
Chasing paper in the breeze,
Picking invites from the ground.

Now the time is getting late,
The sun has fallen in the sky.
Time to go to Sparkle's house.
Stars glimmer as Jess goes by.

Sparkle is a night-time fairy,
Bringing magic to your dreams.
She twinkles like a glistening star
Whilst the moonlight beams and gleams.

Sparkle can help with the party too.
Jess needs stars and fairy lights.
The party will start late afternoon,
She hopes it will last to midnight!

Inside Sparkle's twinkle house
Stars shimmer all around!
They talk, and wish on falling stars.
Sparkle knows where they are all found.

Jess waves goodbye to Sparkle,
It's time to say goodnight.
The moon is out, it's getting cold,
Time for Jessie to take flight!

Sleepily Jessie flutters home.
Tired out, needing to rest.
She dreams of her party when she sleeps,
Sure that it will be the best!

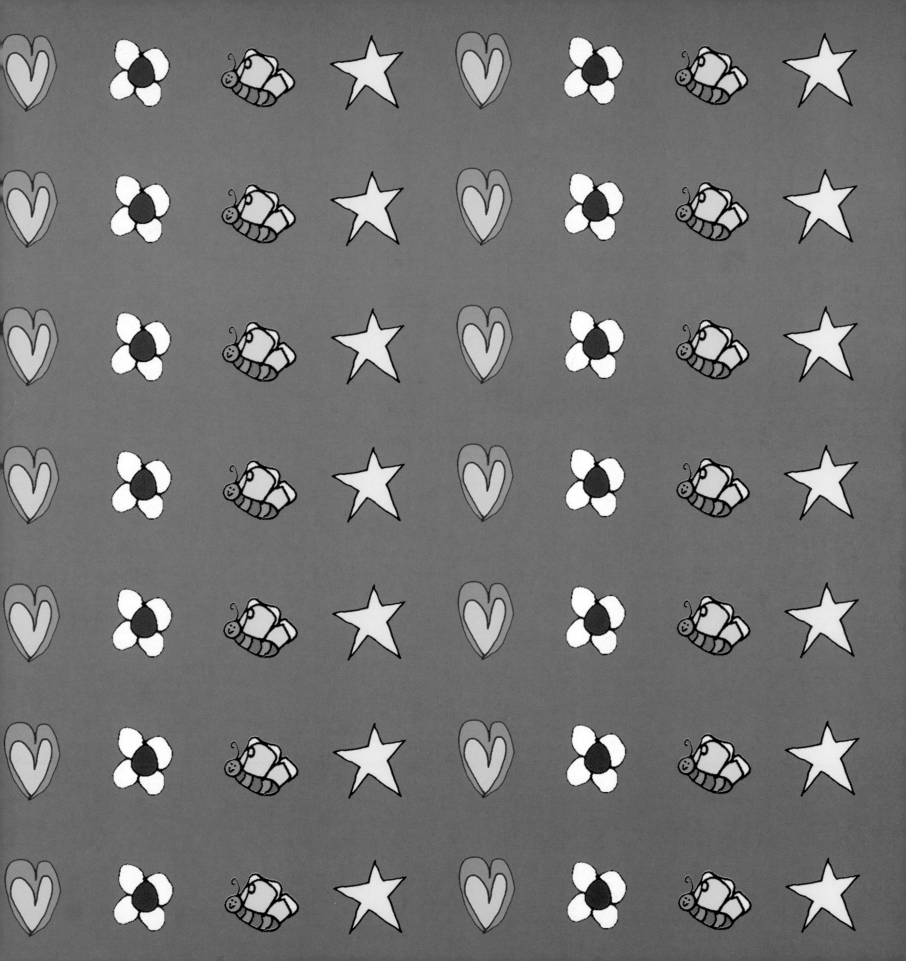

Look Out!

If you liked Fairy Friends,
try these other great Tickle Misses titles:

ISBN 978-1-78244-360-5

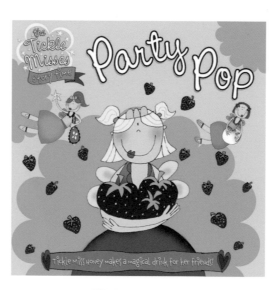

ISBN 978-1-78244-361-2

ISBN 978-1-78244-362-9

Poppy

Sparkle

The
Tickle
Misses

Honey

Jessie